BAREFOOT

THE BAREFOOT didn't see the eyes watching him as he ran onto the overgrown pathway.

His breath came in great gasps. In the hours since he had run from the plantation, he had traveled faster and farther than ever in his life. He was fearful of what lay before him. He was terrified of what lay behind.

The heron's keen eyes had spotted the Barefoot moving furtively toward the pathway. The heron's warning cry had been a signal to the other animals.

They had seen many Barefeet along their pathway. And they had seen some of them being led away in ropes by the Heavy Boots.

The Barefoot stopped and leaned wearily against the trunk of a loblolly pine. He raised a bottle to his lips. It was empty, and no water flowed to his mouth.

Then from a few feet away came the urgent croaking
of a frog. It sang out its message into the night:
"Freshwater. Freshwater."
   The Barefoot moved toward the sound and drank
deeply.

Looking back along the pathway, the Barefoot
made a decision. He sank down in the tall marsh
grass, his head on his arms. There was a rustling
sound. His heart pounding, the Barefoot
slowly raised his head and saw a white-footed
mouse nibbling a wild berry.

The white-footed mouse scurried away as the Barefoot
reached for a handful of berries, stuffing them into his
mouth with a frantic hunger.

From the branches of the cherry tree a mockingbird began to sing. Looking up at the tree, the Barefoot watched a squirrel disappearing into its nest of twigs and leaves.

With an exhausted sigh, the Barefoot pulled a thick blanket of leaves over himself. He closed his eyes and rested.

But the heron, standing sentinel, broke the silence.
His warning cry echoed along the pathway.

The Heavy Boots were closing in on their prey.
It was too late for the Barefoot to find safety.

Loud voices and tramping feet grew nearer.
"We'll get him," cried a voice.
"He'll soon be back where he belongs," laughed another.
One of the Heavy Boots kicked at a rock in his path.

Suddenly out of the grass rose an army of mosquitoes. The Heavy Boots stopped within inches of where the Barefoot lay. Dozens of mosquitoes attacked, biting hands and faces and through clothing.

The Heavy Boots moved away from the marsh grass, slapping and cursing.

Ahead of them a shape darted across the pathway. A cracking of branches brought cries of "There he is," as the Heavy Boots crashed their way into the thick undergrowth.

They cursed again and slashed at greenbrier and poison ivy as the deer led them farther and farther away from where the Barefoot lay trembling.

The mosquitoes returned to their hideaways amid the grass. The mockingbird sang again. The Barefoot looked at his body in awe. Not one mosquito bite was to be seen.

Hidden along the pathway, the animals watched the Barefoot. He walked straighter than before, knowing he had eluded his pursuers.

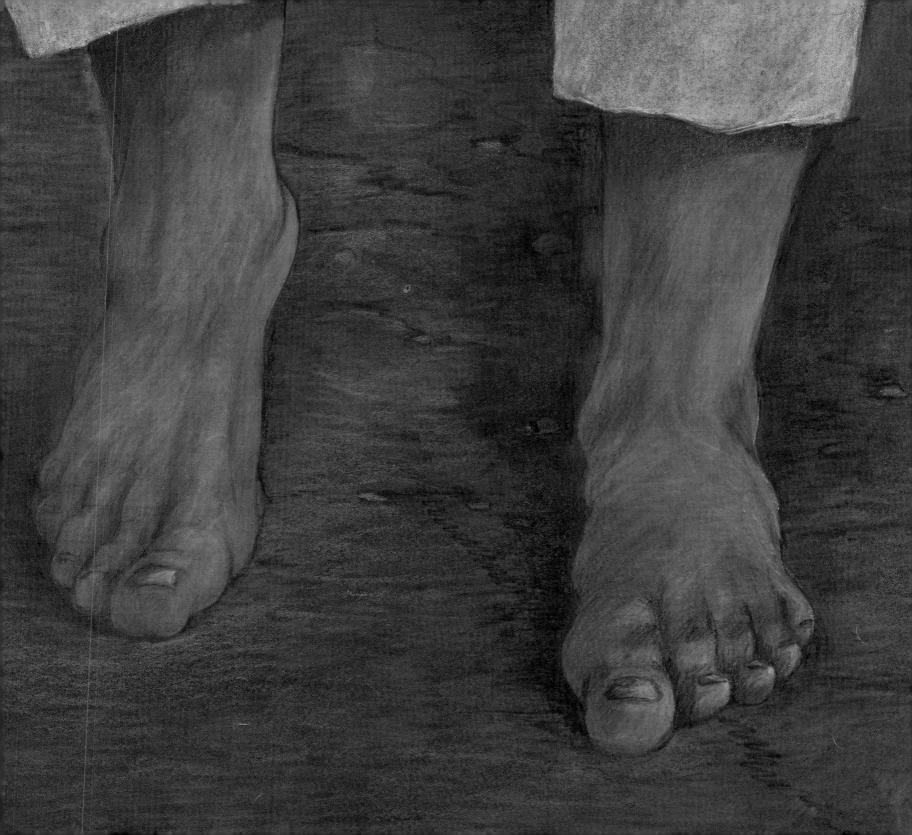

As he reached the quilt, a door opened and a warm light flooded through. With wonder on his face, the Barefoot glanced back at the pathway he had traveled.

He slipped through the door, the noises of the animals following him. To the Barefoot's ears, the sounds were a salute to courage.

The pathway opened out to a wider area. Trees had been felled and logs stacked as if for a fire. Standing a little way off was a house.

The animals heard a quick intake of the Barefoot's breath. Did this house represent safety or danger?

The Barefoot strained to see the house, but the moon remained behind thick clouds.

Then out from the trees flew firefly after firefly.
Their tiny lanterns sparkled and flashed as the Barefoot
moved silently forward. His eyes suddenly made out the

shape of a quilt hanging in front of the house. This was the signal of welcome for which the Barefoot had been hoping.

Silence fell again along the pathway, and the animals slept. But through their dreams the heron's cry once again screamed a warning.

Another Barefoot was approaching.

AUTHOR'S NOTE

The pathway along which the runaway slave in this story traveled was part of the Underground Railroad, a network of courageous people who helped pass runaways from one "safe house" to another northward to freedom. There were many signals used to show a runaway that it was safe to approach a house: special songs, a lantern shining from a particular window, and often a quilt hung over a porch rail or a clothesline. When the Barefoot saw the quilt hanging in front of the house in the clearing, he knew he would be safe until he continued his journey the following night.

Most slaves like the Barefoot had worked in plantation fields at some time. They were familiar with animal signs. The Barefoot knew there must be freshwater nearby when he heard the frog croaking. Of course, the animals had no idea they were helping this brave Barefoot . . . or do you think perhaps they did?